Morristown Centennial Library
Regulations
(802) 888-3853
www.centenniallibrary.org
centenniallib2@yahoo.com

Unless a shorter time is indicated, books and magazines may be borrowed for four weeks, audio books on tape and CD may be borrowed for three weeks, and videos and DVDs may be borrowed for one week. All library materials may be renewed once for the same time period.

A fine of five cents a day every day open will be charged on all overdue library books and audio books. A fine of one dollar a day every day open will be charged for overdue library videos and DVDs.

No library material is to be lent out of the household of the borrower.

All damage to library materials beyond reasonable wear and all losses shall be made good by the borrower.

Library Hours

Sunday & Monday	Closed
Tuesday	9:30am – 7 pm
Wednesday	9:30am – 7pm
Thursday	10am – 5:30pm
Friday	10am – 5:30pm
Saturday	9am – 2pm

Thank You, Mama

Kate Banks   pictures by Gabi Swiatkowska

Frances Foster Books
Farrar Straus Giroux
New York

It was Alice's birthday.

Alice's mama and papa
took her to the zoo.

Alice reached for the balloon.

"Thank you, Papa," said Alice's father.

"Thank you, Papa," said Alice.

"Would you like a birthday hat?" said Alice's mama.

"No," said Alice. "I don't want a hat."

"No, thank you," said Alice's mama.

"No, thank you, Mama," said Alice.

"I would like a pet."

"A pet?" said Alice's papa.
"Would you like a giraffe?"
"No, thank you," said Alice.

"How will I pat its head?"

"What about a tiger?"

said Alice's mama.

"No, thank you," said Alice.

"How will I feed it?"

"**What** about **an** elephant?" said Alice's papa.

"No, thank you," said Alice. "Where will it sleep?"

"What about a parrot?" said Alice.

Alice's parents got her a parrot.

"Thank you, Mama," said Alice.

"Thank you, Papa."

On the way home, Alice's father bought her an ice cream. "Thank you, papa," said Alice.

"Thank you, Papa," said the parrot.

Alice's mother bought her a flower.

"Thank you, Mama," said Alice.

"Thank you, Mama," said the parrot.

When they got home, the parrot was hungry.

"Polly wants a cracker," it said.

Alice gave the parrot a cracker.

"What do you say?" she said.

"Thank you, Mama," said the parrot.

"No. Thank you, Alice," said Alice. "I'm Alice."

"Thank you, Mama," said the parrot.

The parrot was thirsty.

"Polly wants some water."

So Alice gave the parrot a drink.

"What do you say?" she said.

"Thank you, Papa," said the parrot.

"No," said Alice. "Thank you, Alice."

"Thank you, Papa,"
said the parrot again.
Alice frowned.

When bedtime came, Alice's mother asked,

"Did you have a nice birthday, Alice?"
"Yes, thank you, Mama," said Alice.

Alice's father gave her a kiss.

"Thank you, Papa,"

said Alice.

"Polly wants a kiss,"
said the parrot.

So Alice leaned over and
kissed the parrot on the head.

"What do you say?"
Alice said.

"Thank you, Alice," said the parrot. "Thank you, Alice."

And Alice kissed the parrot again.

Farrar Straus Giroux Books for Young Readers
175 Fifth Avenue, New York 10010

Color separations by Bright Arts (H.K.) Ltd.
Printed in China by South China Printing Co. Ltd.,
Dongguan City, Guangdong Province
Designed by Jay Colvin
First edition, 2013
1 3 5 7 9 10 8 6 4 2

mackids.com

Library of Congress Cataloging-in-Publication Data
Banks, Kate, 1960–
    Thank you, Mama / Kate Banks ; pictures by Gabi Swiatkowska. — 1st ed.
      p.   cm.
    Summary: Alice's parents get her a parrot for her birthday.
    ISBN 978-0-374-37444-0 (hardcover)
    [1. Birthdays—Fiction.   2. Parrots—Fiction.]   I. Swiatkowska, Gabi,
ill.   II. Title.

PZ7.B22594Th 2013
[E]—dc23

2012028795